Wake up, raccoon.

Wake up, bat.
Say "Hello" to the moon.

Wake up, cricket.

Wake up, firefly.

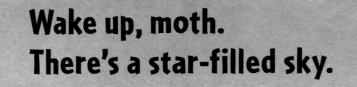

Wake up, moth.
There's a star-filled sky.

Wake up, porcupine.

Wake up, mouse.

It's nighttime, mole.
Come out of your house.

The stars are out. The moon is bright.
Wake up, creatures of the night!
It's your time to fly or walk or leap.

But it's my time to go to sleep.